Flower Fairies™
Art
Activity
Book

Have you ever seen a fairy? Next time you are wandering about in your garden, or the park, look very closely. You might be lucky enough to spot some fluttering wings out of the corner of your eye. It doesn't matter if the sun is shining, or rain is pouring down, every tree, flower and plant you see will have a fairy to look after it. There will be fairies dancing in the meadows, fairies playing in the quiet wood, and fairies resting by the babbling stream.

There are lots of Flower Fairies waiting to meet you inside this book. Pick out your most fabulous colors and bring them to life. There are fairies for you to draw too, as well as plenty of activities and games. Plus a pretty sticker sheet to help you complete your loveliest pictures. Just spread your wings and let your imagination soar. Don't forget to shower the fairies with fairy dust too!

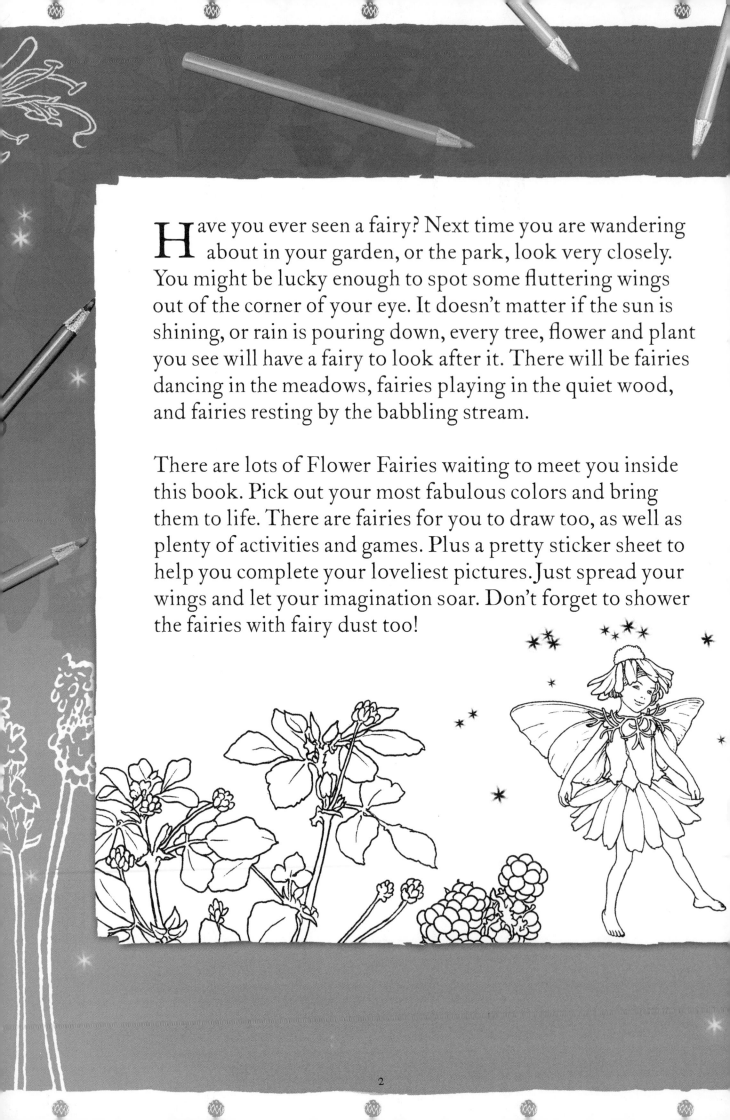

Spring

Spring is when all the Flower Fairies stretch out their new shoots and bask in the first rays of warm sunshine.

Look at all the fairies that have appeared with the new season! Color them in using lots of bright greens, reds and yellows. When you have finished you could draw a big sun in the sky.

Summer

Summer is a time for basking in the hot sunshine, picnics in the meadow and refreshing dips in the cool stream.

It's very hot today. Can you help these fairies keep cool in the shade by drawing a tree with big branches for them to play under? The grassy meadow they are in is full of wild flowers in every color. Can you draw them into the picture?

Fall

The nights are beginning to draw in and there is less time for play.

These fairies are rushing through the rain to reach the Bonfire Festival. Soon they will be warm and dry, enjoying delicious cups of sweet blackberry cordial.

Can you help keep them dry on their journey by drawing umbrellas above them? Perhaps they would be made from big leaves? You could add some star stickers too to help the fairies find their way.

Winter

During winter, everything slows down in the garden and the meadow. It's hard for things to grow when it's cold and the ground is icy hard.

Although it's freezing outside, everyone is warm inside Nightshade Berry's cozy home. Some of the fairies have got together to sip sorrel soup and get clothes ready for the spring. Can you decorate the walls with pictures? Add some tables, chairs, dishes and cups. Perhaps there are lamps or a fire?

This is Kingcup and some little elves.

Find lots of shades of yellow and gold to color them in.

Pansies come in all sorts of bright colors so choose your favorites and bring the Pansy Fairy to life.

Would you like to be able to draw the Fuchsia Fairy?

Copy the contents of each square carefully onto the empty grid opposite.

Now color in both pictures in shades of pink and purple.

Each spring the Nasturtium Fairy plants new things in his garden. What do you think he will plant this year?

Color him in and draw some flowers and plants in his empty pots. You could add some flower stickers too!

The pretty Zinnia Fairy is all set to spring clean her home, but what do you think her home looks like?

Color Zinnia in, then draw her home behind her. Is it made from a toadstool? Use some leaf stickers to help make it cozy.

It's a blustery spring morning and there is lots of washing and drying in Flower Fairyland.

Draw some fairy clothes onto this line. You could draw your favorite clothes on there too!

Look at this picture carefully then see if you can write the right word for each space in the sentences below.
Now color the picture in.

The poor _____ has his leg in a bandage.

The brown _____ has hurt her tail.

The fairy is wearing a red _____ on his head.

Flower Fairies have beautiful wings which help them to swoop and glide from flower to flower.

Can you draw a pair of gorgeous wings onto this fairy? Why not sprinkle some fairy dust over him too?

You will need to find lots of yellow, gold and green shades to color the beautiful Iris Fairy.

The Double Daisy Fairy has tiny little flowers, but they are easy to spot in the flowerbed as they are bright red!

Look very carefully at the groups of flowers and leaves below. Can you carry on the sequence by working out which flower or leaf to draw at the end of each line?

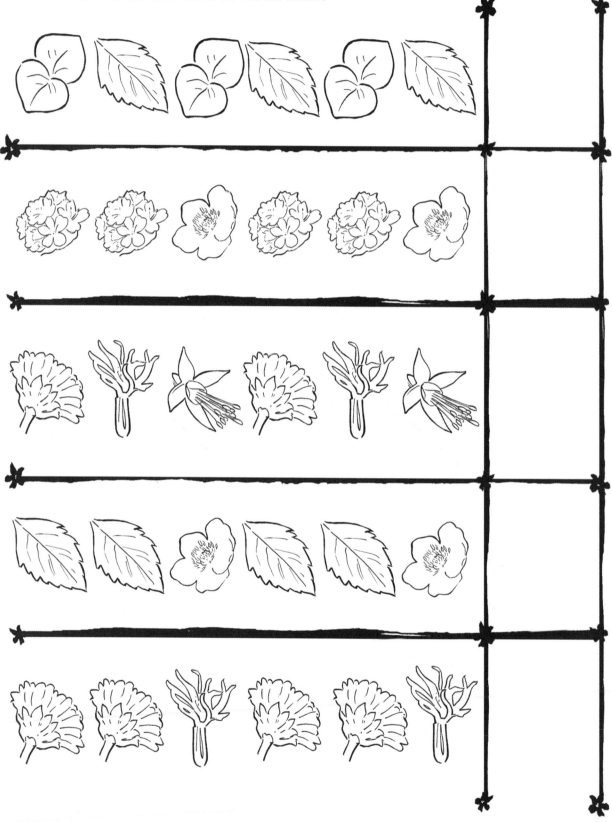

Now brighten everything up with some color.

There's lots to color in this picture of two marching
Flower Fairies.

Starting at number one, join the dots together until the Ragged Robin Fairy is completely revealed. Then color him in.

What kind of fairy would wear this skirt? Can you create your own fairy by drawing some arms, legs, a head and some wings?

If one fairy wants to send a secret message to another, they can use the secret fairy code.

meet	the	by	meadow	a
on	rose	me	in	of
garden	for	dancing	please	picnic
daffodil	cakes	come	party	you

Can you unscramble this note by using the code cracker above?

_____ _____ _____ _____

_____ _____ _____ _____

If you've ever walked down a sunny lane in spring, you will have seen the Primrose Fairy's flowers.

Join the dots, starting at one.

Here is the Apple Blossom fairy. Apples grow in autumn, but in spring the trees are covered with pretty blossom. Use your palest colors to finish this picture.

The pretty Tansy Fairy loves to sew. Can you bring her to life with some bright shades of yellow and green?

Heather grows up on the hills during the warmer months.

Brighten up this picture with some pinks and purples.

This fairy's flowers grow everywhere during the summer, and they are the color of sunshine!

Join the dots, starting at one, then color the picture.

If the weather is warm, it's fun to share a picnic with friends.
What do you think these fairies would like to eat and drink?

Add the fairy stickers from the center of the book, then draw
in your favorite foods. You could add some apple stickers too!

The Columbine Fairy looks so pretty in her pink and
yellow dress.

Draw her by copying the contents of each square carefully onto
the empty grid opposite.

Now color in both pictures.

Join the dots, starting at one, to complete the musical Bugle Fairy. Color him in using shades of blue and purple.

38

1. Peach   2. Pink   3. Green   4. Red

This picture uses lots of pretty colors. Use the color key to help bring the picture to life.

What kinds of flowers and trees grow in your park or garden?
Draw and color some of the things you see in the space below.

Now add the fairies from the sticker sheet to complete the
lovely scene.

Finally, create a border for your picture using stickers.

Almond Blossom is in a hurry. It's the Midsummer Floral Feast and she can't wait! Help her find a way through the maze so she isn't late.

Now color all the pictures, and draw flowers along the path that
leads to the feast to help other fairies find their way.

Cornflowers are deep blue like sky in midsummer.

Color the blooms and then find a lighter shade for his wings.

1. Brown

2. Cream

3. Green

4. Lavender

Mmm, Lavender smells gorgeous.

The little Strawberry Fairy has lots of sweet, juicy berries for you. Can you finish the picture by drawing more strawberries, leaves and flowers?

A	B	C	D	R	A	G	O	N	F	L	Y	F
E	N	Y	H	A	B	C	D	E	G	E	L	F
A	B	C	D	E	F	G	H	A	D	E	F	L
E	Y	H	A	B	G	F	D	E	G	F	R	L
A	B	B	I	R	D	R	H	A	D	E	E	F
E	E	N	Y	H	C	E	E	G	F	G	T	G
A	E	C	E	G	F	P	H	A	D	E	T	L
E	S	H	A	B	B	P	D	E	G	R	U	L
A	B	C	F	E	F	O	C	D	E	G	B	L
E	E	N	R	H	C	H	E	P	F	G	L	B
A	Y	E	O	Y	H	S	P	F	E	G	L	G
E	N	Y	G	A	B	S	D	E	G	F	G	L
E	N	Y	H	E	H	A	H	A	B	G	F	O
E	N	Y	H	S	B	R	D	E	G	E	G	F
A	B	C	S	C	D	G	G	E	S	U	O	M

BIRD   DRAGONFLY   FROG

BEE   BUTTERFLY   MOUSE

GRASSHOPPER

Flower Fairies share their world with lots of different creatures. Can you find their names inside this box of letters? Their names are written underneath to help you.

The scent of Honeysuckle is gorgeous, and the blooms are a beautiful yellow and pink color.

You may not be able to smell these flowers, but you could make them look very pretty.

pages 17 and 52

pages 40-41

pages 40-41 (border

page 58

pages 34-35

pages 94-95

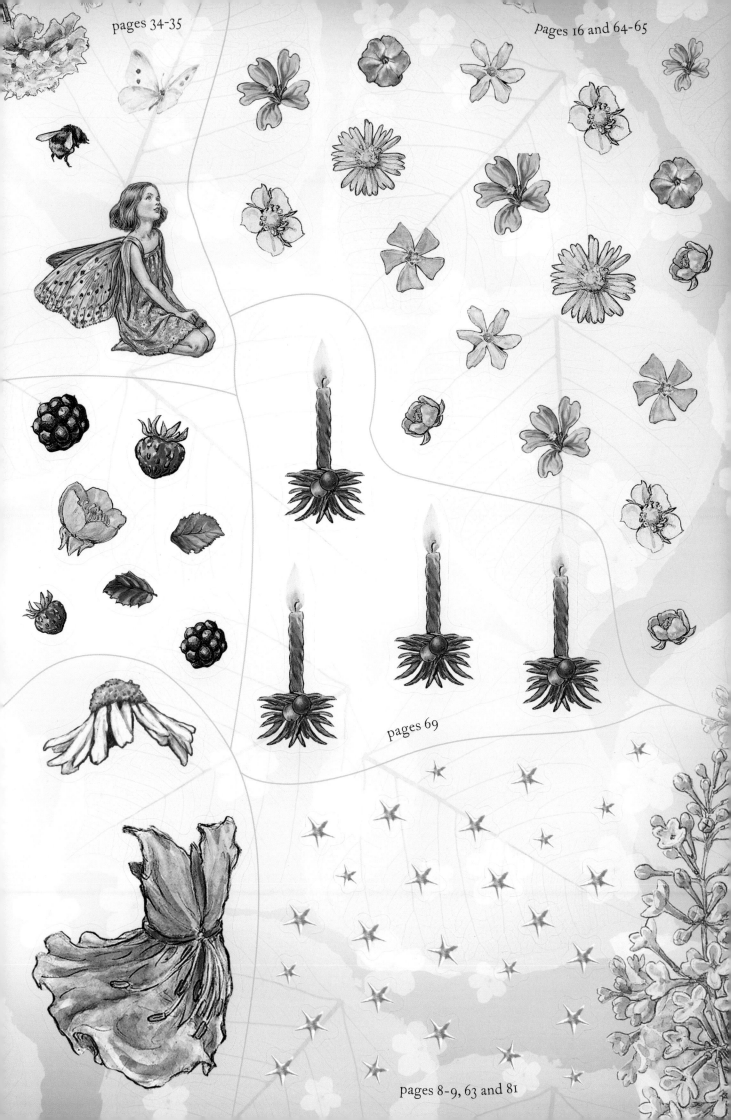

pages 34-35

pages 16 and 64-65

pages 69

pages 8-9, 63 and 81

Tulips come in lots of bright shades. See how bright you can make these ones.

Look at the glossy berries that belong to this fairy.

Find lots of red and purple shades to brighten up this picture of the Wayfaring Tree Fairy.

The Silver Birch Fairy has an orange fall skirt.
She loves to swing from her delicate branches.

During fall, leaves of all shapes and sizes fall from the trees. Can you finish this picture by copying some of the leaves?

Add some leaf stickers too. Finally, maybe you'd like to add some sparkling raindrops!

The Gorse Fairies are such good friends, despite their spikes!
Can you color in this beautiful picture ?

Can you create a fall garden scene with your pencils? Then find some real leaves to add on if you can!

Does your garden have tall trees, blowing leaves, blackberry bushes, and brown conkers on the ground?

Complete this picture of the Eyebright fairy.

Now color him in using shades of pink and yellow.

Color in the smiling Nightshade Berry Fairy.

His glossy berries are green, red and yellow.

Carefully color in the apple tree. Add as many apples as you like.
You could add some stickers too!

1.
Peach

2.
Pink

3.
Green

4.
Brown

Follow the color code to bring this picture of the Bee Orchis Fairy to life.

Have a good look at the line below.
What do you think it could be?

Add some more lines and turn it into a picture. It could be you as
a fairy perhaps! What color would your pretty dress be?

Have you seen the fall fruits and foliage below?

Work out what comes next, to solve the patterns below.

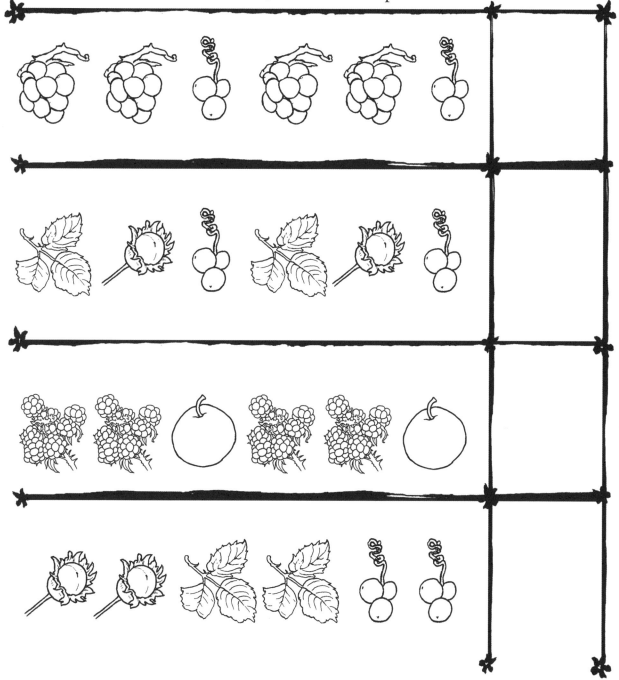

Now brighten everything up with some color.

There is a fairy hiding among all these shapes.
Can you spot him?

Color in the shapes that contain a grey flower and he will
be revealed!

The Nasturtium Fairy is using a leaf as an umberella. Can you draw some raindrops and add some star stickers?

Jasmine has a very strong scent.

As you color in this picture imagine you are smelling the most gorgeous perfume you can imagine! Add some flower stickers too to make a beautiful picture.

Here is a lovely rhyme all about a flower coming to life in the spring. Can you find the missing words to complete the rhyme by choosing them from the box underneath?

The _____ of _____ are keen and _____;

I fear them not, for I am _____.

My _____ flowers are brave and bright;

I greet the _____ with all my might!

bold   yellow

spring   winds

March   cold

Next time you are in the garden or the park, have a good look at all the different shaped petals you can see. Can you draw some in the space below? Are they long? Short? Round? Add some stickers too.

My Petals

The Black Medick Fairy is teaching her little brother all about
their pretty yellow flowers. Color the scene in.

It's Christmas time at last! Can you color in the fairy at the top of the tree and then add some pretty decorations?

This naughty little fairy is chasing the Burdock Fairy.

Color them in before they run away!

What would you do if you were a Flower Fairy for the day? Let your imagination soar as you fill in the spaces below.

Dear _____

I have had such a busy day today! This morning I flew high over the _____ to visit the _____ Fairy. She invited me into her little _____ and poured me a delicious cup of fresh _____ cordial. She had baked some _____ too. They were very tasty.

Love from _____

These fairies are off to the far side of the Bluebell Wood for a dancing lesson, but how will they get there? They are missing their wings! Find your most beautiful colors to draw some and help them fly away.

Look at this smiley fairy.

Color him in using lots of wintery shades of red and green.

Join the dots, starting at number one, to finish this picture of the Lily-of-the-Valley Fairy. Now color the picture using delicate green shades.

Look at all the pretty fairies! Color them in however you like, and draw yourself and a friend in the space.

What kind of wings and dress would you wear if you were a
Flower Fairy? Would they be sparkling?

All the fairies have been looking forward to the magical
Winter Ball, but the fairies above have nothing to wear!

Can you design an outfit for each one? Then add some stickers
to make the picture really bright.

It's late at night and these fairies will soon be heading back to their flowerbeds to sleep.

Color them in and add some star stickers to the sky so they will
be able to find their way home.

Color in the spikey Thistle Fairy. Find a rich purple color for
the flowers.

The Winter Jasmine Fairy brings a bright splash of yellow
to cold winter days.

Help Apple Blossom write to her friend Tulip by filling in the blank words.

Dear Tulip

Today I have been teaching my little brother how to _____. He is very nervous and we have spent all morning sitting on a _____! His wings are very new and he is not quite brave enough to _____. Although it was nice sitting in the _____ it would have been much nice to go flying with _____!

Lots of _____,
Apple Blossom

you   love
sunshine   jump
fly   branch

Look at the fairy names below. Can you find the missing letters for each space? Some helpful fairies are holding up the right letters, you just have to work out which one fits where.

BLUE _ ELL

_ OSE

BU _ TERCUP

The first blooms of spring have been spotted down by the stream. Which fairy saw them first? Follow them along the petal path to find out.

3rd

1st

2nd

This fairy is stocking up his pantry.
Look at the list and help him by drawing extra
things on the shelves so that he has the
right amount of tasty treats for the
cold winter months ahead.

3 strawberries
4 acorns
2 cherries
6 rosehips
3 apples

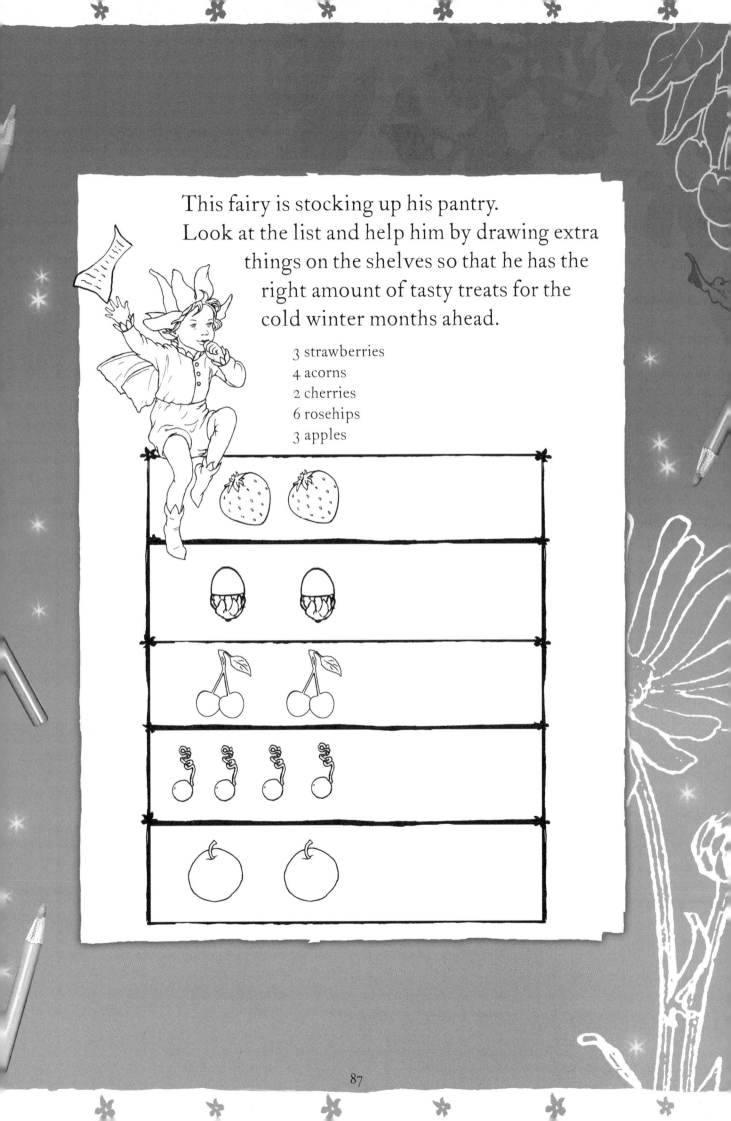

There is something magical about a fairy in flight and it's not so difficult to draw.

Carefully copy the contents of each square onto the empty grid opposite.

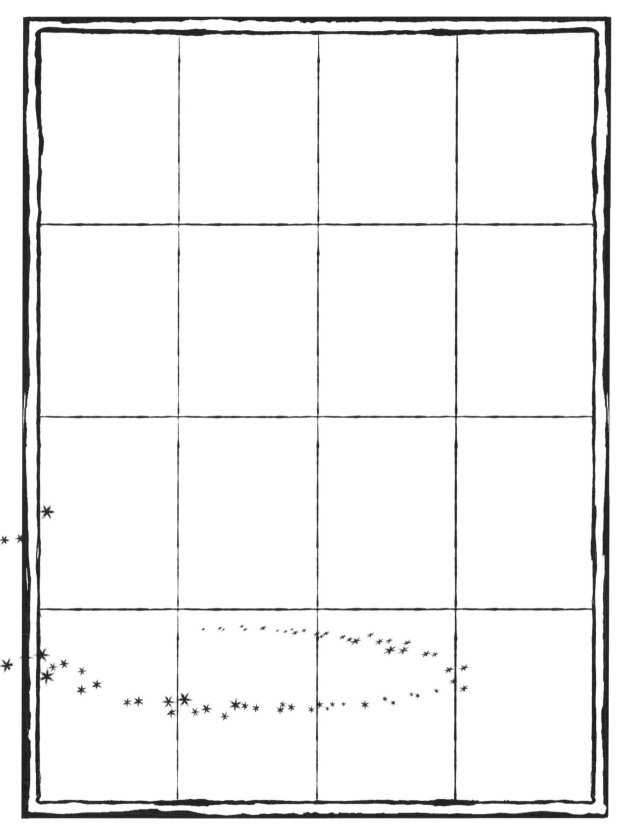

Now color the picture, and most importantly of all, sprinkle some sparkles over her wings to help her fly high!

Here is an exciting drawing game to play with a friend. All you need is a pencil and dice.

How to play: The aim is to draw a fairy like the one below as quickly as possible, and beat your opponent! To start, each player throws the dice alternately until someone throws a one. This player can then draw a fairy head. The other player continues until they too throw a one while the first player must throw a two, then a three, etc. and draw their fairy as shown below. The first person to finish their picture is the winner! When you've finished, why not color your fairies in?

- [•] Head
- [Body]
- [Arms]
- [Legs]
- [Wings]
- [Tiara]

Player 1

Player 2

How much do you know about your favorite friendly Flower Fairies? See if you can complete the sentences by choosing the correct word from the box below.

needle   Rose   tree   thread   white

The _____ Fairy is pink
and smells gorgeous!
The butterflies that flutter around
the garden are _____ .
Pretty Apple Blossom sits in a
_____ with her baby brother.
Tansy stitches beautifully with
a tiny _____
and _____ .

Do you think all these pictures look the same? Study them very carefully and see if you can spot and circle five differences.

These poor fairies do not look very magical at all.
Can you help them? Add the stickers of their pretty
dresses. One of the fairies has a hat too!

Now find some fabulous bits and pieces such as floaty fabric, shiny paper and glitter to stick on. They need some wings and maybe some shoes or a tiara.

The Holly Fairy has come to say goodbye.

His deep red berries look so colorful against the bright white of a glittering snowy day.